BIONICLE™

Trial
by Fire

BIONICLE™

FIND THE POWER,
LIVE THE LEGEND

The legend comes alive in these exciting BIONICLE™ books:

BIONICLE™ Chronicles

#1 Tale of the Toa
#2 Beware the Bohrok
#3 Makuta's Revenge
#4 Tales of the Masks

The Official Guide to BIONICLE™

BIONICLE™ Collector's Sticker Book

BIONICLE™: Mask of Light

BIONICLE™ Adventures

#1 Mystery of Metru Nui

BIONICLE™

Trial by Fire

by Greg Farshtey

SCHOLASTIC INC.
New York Toronto London Auckland Sydney
Mexico City New Delhi Hong Kong Buenos Aires

For Heidi, my best friend
and a true joy to know

ISBN 0-439-60732-9

12 11 10 9 8 7 6 5 4   4 5 6 7 8/0

Printed in the U.S.A.
First printing, April 2004

'05
BY

The City of Metru Nui

BIONICLE

Trial
by Fire

PROLOGUE

Tahu Nuva, Toa of Fire, struggled to accept all that he had heard. Many a time he had listened to Turaga Vakama, elder of the village of Ta-Koro, tell a tale of past glories. But never such a story as this.

He had asked the Turaga to share with him and his fellow heroes a tale of Metru Nui. The Toa would soon be leading the Matoran villagers to this new island. They wished to be prepared for any danger that might await them there.

The tale Vakama told was a shocking one. He revealed that he and the other village elders had, long ago, been Matoran, living in a great city on Metru Nui. Through a strange twist of fate, they were gifted with the power of Toa. Their destiny: to save their city from disaster.

"We believed Metru Nui to be a paradise," Vakama had said. "But it was a city under siege. A dark, twisted plant called the Morbuzakh threatened from every side, bringing down buildings and driving Matoran from their homes. If left unchecked, nothing would remain of the city we loved."

But how to save the city? The answer came to Vakama in a vision. The Toa Metru had to seek out six Matoran who knew the hiding places of the Great Disks. These disks, when used together, could defeat the Morbuzakh. It seemed a simple task, and one that would surely prove to all in Metru Nui that these new Toa were worthy of being called heroes.

But the six Toa faced many dangers before the Matoran could be found. Still unskilled in the use of their powers, they barely escaped traps that had been set along their way. It soon became clear that one of the Matoran was seeking to betray the others, and all of Metru Nui as well.

It was at that point that Vakama had

stopped speaking. Now the Toa had gathered again to hear more of his strange tale.

Gali Nuva, Toa of Water, approached him quietly and laid a hand on his shoulder.

"Are you ready to continue, Turaga?" she asked. "Should we wait for another time?"

Vakama shook his head. "No, Toa Gali. These secrets have been kept from you for far too long. The time has come to speak. But . . . it is not easy."

"You said that you felt sure one of the six Matoran was walking in shadow," Tahu, Toa of Fire, said. "Why didn't you turn him over to the enforcers of order in Metru Nui — what did you call them?"

"Vahki," replied Vakama. "We had no choice. Those six Matoran were the only ones who knew the location of the Great Disks, and we had to have those disks. But we knew we must take precautions against betrayal."

"Tell us more, Turaga," said Pohatu. "Continue your story, please."

"Very well, Toa of Stone," said Vakama. "Now where was I? Oh, yes. With the six Matoran having been found, we Toa Metru were ready to begin searching for the Great Disks. Time was running out — with each day, the Morbuzakh grew bolder and more of the city was brought to ruin.

"It was decided that we would split into teams to search the city for the disks, bringing the Matoran with us. Of course, not everyone was happy about this idea. . . ."

"Next time, I'm picking the teams," grumbled Onewa, Toa Metru of Stone. He had been trudging along behind Vakama, Toa of Fire, and two of the Matoran for the better part of an hour. He hadn't bothered to keep his unhappiness a secret.

Nuhrii said nothing. A Matoran from the Ta-Metru district, all his energies were focused on finding the disks. In his mind, he saw himself showered with praise for helping to save the city and maybe even having a Mask of Power named after him someday. Turaga Dume, elder of Metru Nui, might even want a Matoran of such courage as an advisor.

The other Matoran on the journey, Ahkmou, was a Po-Matoran carver. He turned back to look at Onewa and said, "Since when did Onewa follow the rules? Has becoming a Toa

Metru made you soft? Leave these two fire-spitters behind and let's find the Great Disk ourselves."

"Sure," grunted Onewa. "And maybe walk into another trap. Don't think I've forgotten how hard it was to catch you, Ahkmou. I trust you about as far as I could throw the Great Temple."

Vakama was tempted to tell the bickering Po-Metru natives to be quiet, but that would probably just make things worse. Maybe it had been a mistake using Kanoka disks to choose the teams. But they were easy to find, since every Matoran used disks for sport, and the three-digit codes on them offered a simple way to decide. The two lowest codes worked together, the two highest, and so on. It was just bad luck he had wound up with Onewa. They just could not seem to get along.

They had crossed the border of Ta-Metru a short while ago. Nokama, Toa Metru of Water, had found a series of clues to the locations of the Great Disks carved on the wall of the Great Temple. According to the inscription, finding the

Ta-Metru disk required "embracing the root of fire." Vakama and Nuhrii both knew what that meant, but neither wanted to speak about it out loud.

Onewa and Ahkmou looked around, uncomfortably. Their home metru was known for its wide, flat expanses where massive sculptures were carved and stored. Ta-Metru, on the other hand, was a land of fire, where molten rivers of protodermis were forged into masks, tools, and other objects. Buildings crowded in close and all of them reflected the red glow of the furnaces. The sound of crafters' tools striking in unison and the hiss of cooling masks seemed to come from every side.

"I need a rest," said Ahkmou. "My feet are tired."

"Mine too," said Nuhrii. "Why couldn't we just take the transport chutes?"

Vakama frowned. He had insisted that they travel on foot, and Onewa had agreed. Taking the chutes would make it too easy for one or both Matoran to jump out midway and disappear into the streets and alleyways. "All right. But stay to-gether and stay here."

The two Matoran sat down. Vakama walked away, expecting Onewa to keep an eye on them, but the Toa Metru of Stone followed him. "Do you know where we're going? What is this 'root of fire'?"

Vakama gestured toward the buildings that surrounded them. "Well, you know about the Great Furnace in Ta-Metru, and all the smaller furnaces and forges here. The flames that feed them come from fire pits . . . the 'roots' of the fire. They are highly dangerous places."

"Let me guess. Climbing down into one is against the law in Ta-Metru, so we're going to have Vahki squads to worry about."

"Probably."

"You had better be right about all this," Onewa said. "Or it's the last time I'm trusting you, fire-spitter."

Vakama felt anger rising in him, and this time didn't try to fight it off. "Do you have a better plan? These six disks are the only thing that can save Metru Nui. Unless we find them, the whole place is going to fall to the — Morbuzakh!"

The Toa Metru of Fire pointed over Onewa's shoulder, but his warning came too late. A twisted Morbuzakh vine snaked out of a chute and wrapped itself around Onewa, lifting the startled Toa into the air.

"My arms are pinned!" the Toa Metru of Stone shouted. "I can't get free!"

"Hang on! I'll save you!" Vakama said, thrusting a disk into his disk launcher.

"Hang on? Hang on to what??" The Morbuzakh was dragging Onewa toward the chute. Once inside, it would be too late to free him.

Vakama aimed carefully and launched his disk at the vine. When it struck, it sent bitter cold along the length of the plant, freezing it solid. With the pressure gone, Onewa was able to wriggle free. He hit the ground and looked from the vine to Vakama.

"Yeah, well," he muttered. "I could have done that myself . . . somehow." He idly swung his fist and shattered the frozen plant into a thousand icy shards.

Vakama turned and headed back toward where the Matoran waited. "You can have the next one then. Maybe if you grumble at it, it will go away."

"Hasn't worked with you," replied Onewa.

Vakama didn't answer. The spot where they had left Nuhrii and Ahkmou was empty. He felt a sinking feeling inside. If the two of them had vanished . . .

"There!" yelled Onewa. He pointed toward the two Matoran, who were fleeing in the direction of Po-Metru. The Toa of Stone whirled his proto-piton tool above his head and made a perfect throw, the cable wrapping around Ahkmou's legs. Smiling, Onewa began reeling in the Po-Matoran.

"Nice," said Vakama. "But here's an easier way." He took out a teleportation disk, checked its three-digit code to make sure it was low power, and then hurled it from his launcher. It struck Nuhrii a glancing blow and the Ta-Matoran disappeared. An instant later, he popped back into existence right in front of the two Toa.

"I guess you weren't that tired after all," said Vakama. "So let's keep moving."

"So have you ever visited these fire pits before?" Onewa asked.

"No," Vakama said softly. "Even mask makers are not allowed near them. The risk is too great."

"Scorched Matoran, right?"

"Not only that," said Vakama. "If anything happened to the flames in those pits, production in Ta-Metru would come to a halt." Seeing the lack of reaction on Onewa's face, he added, "There would be nothing for the Po-Matoran to carve."

They were working their way slowly toward the center of the city, trying to keep off the busier avenues. Onewa insisted the two Matoran stay close, while he himself kept scanning the alleys. Vakama did not need to ask why. They both could sense they were being followed.

At one point, just after they rounded a corner, Onewa gestured for them to flatten against the wall. They waited a long moment, but no one went by except the occasional Matoran. Finally, Onewa peered around the edge of the building and shook his head. "Not there."

"Who do you think it is?" asked Ahkmou.

"Guess," answered Onewa. A four-legged creature named Nidhiki had been chasing Ahkmou when Onewa found him. The same powerful being had been responsible for sabotage and traps encountered by the other Toa Metru in their search for the Matoran. Whoever he was, he did not want the Toa finding the Great Disks.

"Maybe we should get off the street," Vakama suggested. "We can take a shortcut through —"

"The protodermis reclamation furnace," Nuhrii finished. "The rear exit would bring us out near the fire pits."

"Lead the way," said Onewa. "All these fires, flames, and furnaces look alike to me."

* * *

The protodermis reclamation furnace was relatively small as Ta-Metru furnaces went, but its fires were just as hot and had plenty to burn. Damaged masks, tools and other items were sent here from the reclamation yard to be melted down. The resulting liquid protodermis was then fed through special channels back to the forges, where it could be used again. What went into the furnace was little more than garbage, but what came out might become something wonderful in the hands of a skilled crafter.

Its function made it ideal for use as a shortcut to the fire pits. For one thing, the place ran itself. Few, if any, Matoran actually worked there, so the building would most likely be empty. The Nuurakh, the Ta-Metru Vahki squads, did not bother patrolling in the area. After all, who would want to steal trash?

Vakama led the way as they slipped into the side entrance. The only light inside came from the fire in the furnace. The building consisted of a wide catwalk that ran along all four sides and looked down upon a long chute. The chute ran through the center of the building, carrying items directly from the yards to the flames. The air inside was heavy with smoke and the smell of melting protodermis.

Onewa walked to the edge of the catwalk and peered down. He had never seen anything like this. In his home district of Po-Metru, goods arrived already shaped, and carvers added the finishing touches. Watching masks and tools move slowly through a chute toward destruction was incredible, and even a little frightening.

Vakama joined him. "Sometimes I am not sure I like this place."

"Why not?"

"It keeps us from learning from our mistakes. We just melt them down and make them go away."

"Toa! Watch out!"

Neither Vakama nor Onewa had time to react to Nuhrii's shout. Twin blasts of energy struck them, sending them tumbling over the catwalk and through the energized walls of the chute. They hit hard and lay there, stunned, as the chute moved them closer and closer to the white-hot flames.

Nidhiki stepped out of the shadows. The two Matoran had run away, but there would be time to find them later. For now, he wanted to enjoy his victory over the two Toa Metru. He looked down at the unmoving forms of Vakama and Onewa, his dark laughter mingling with the crackling of the flames.

Nuju, Toa Metru of Ice, and Whenua, Toa Metru of Earth, moved slowly and quietly down a darkened corridor. All around them, eyes frozen in suspended animation seemed to watch their progress. The most fearsome creatures ever to appear in Metru Nui were preserved here in the Onu-Metru Archives, still-living exhibits to be studied by Matoran scholars.

Toa Nuju scowled as they walked through the latest in a series of seemingly endless hall-ways, filled with dusty display cases. Before he became a Toa, Nuju's job had been scanning the skies searching for hints of what the future held for Metru Nui. To him, the Archives were nothing but a monument to a dead past.

"I never knew this place was so big," he muttered.

"As big as it needs to be," replied Whenua,

with pride in his voice. "We've added two new sub-levels lately. The subterranean sections will someday stretch to the sea in every direction!"

"Why stop there? Why not just knock down the rest of the metru and turn the whole city into a dusty museum?"

Whenua glanced at Nuju with an expression of irritation. "That might be better than wasting time and space trying to predict tomorrows that might not come."

Nuju shook his head. They had been having some version of this argument since they left Ga-Metru on their search for the Great Disks. Neither one was going to change the other's mind, so there was no future in continuing. "Let's say we both live in the present for a moment. Do you think it was wise to leave Tehutti and Ehrye up above? What if they run off?"

"We left them in a section of the Archives that Tehutti had never visited before. Even the best Matoran archivist would get lost trying to find his way out of an unfamiliar wing, and he knows it. Oh, look at that! We found that insectoid arm digging sub-level 6. It's not Bohrok, but we're not sure what else it might have belonged to."

Nuju smiled. It was probably too much to ask to expect Whenua to stop giving tours. Even in the face of danger — the city threatened by the Morbuzakh plant, a handful of Matoran holding the key to its defeat — Whenua was still an old archivist at heart.

The carving at the Great Temple had advised that "no door must be left unopened" in Onu-Metru if the Great Disk were to be found. But the Archives contained hundreds of thousands of doors, if not more. Fortunately, Tehutti knew which level concealed the disk. Now the trick was finding it.

The two Toa Metru turned a corner. Before them, the hallway stretched as far as the eye could see. Each side was lined with doors easily four times the height of a Toa. The doors were thick and strong, too, and locked tight.

"Why all the locks?" Nuju asked. "Worried someone will break into the exhibits?"

Whenua chuckled. "No, Nuju. Worried that the exhibits will break *out.* Some of these creatures seem able to resist our efforts to put them in stasis."

The Toa Metru of Earth stopped at the first door on the left. No sign gave a hint of what lay behind it, but that wasn't unusual. One of the rules of the Archives was, "If you have to ask what's behind the door, you aren't meant to open it."

Nuju craned his neck to see the top of the massive door, then examined the equally over-sized lock. "I don't suppose you have a key?"

"No. Only the Chief Archivist has keys to this level. If he knew we were rummaging around down here, the Vahki would already be on their way."

Nuju raised his crystal spike and fired a blast of ice at the lock, freezing it solid. "Then we make our own."

Whenua nodded and revved up one of his earthshock drills. It took only a brief touch to shatter the frozen lock.

The door slowly swung open. Nuju peered

inside. "Whenua? There is something in there. Much too big to be a Great Disk."

Before either of them could move, a gigantic Ussal crab claw shot from inside the room and clamped itself around the Toa. "Unngh! Wrong room! Wrong room!" Whenua shouted.

"I figured that out for myself," Nuju replied, straining against the mighty claw to no effect. He was secretly grateful that it was impossible to see the Ussal to which the claw belonged. This day had already had enough nasty surprises.

"This — owww! — is a very rare creature!" Whenua said. "Try not to hurt it!"

Nuju pitted every bit of his strength against the claw and didn't so much as loosen its grip. "We are rare creatures, too, Whenua. Right now, I would even say endangered!"

Whenua activated both of his earthshock drills, setting them spinning at a high rate of speed. "I think I have an idea, but it might bring the whole place down on us."

"Let me worry about the future," Nuju replied. "It's what I do best."

Whenua closed his eyes and concentrated on his Toa tools. The earthshock drills could bore through virutally any substance, even at low speed. But they had one other feature: when in use, they produced a loud hum.

If I can get them going fast enough, he thought. *Hit just the right frequency, maybe . . .*

The drills became a blur, whirling faster and faster. The hum went from painfully loud into the ultrasonic range. Whenua and Nuju both felt certain their heads would split open. Cracks began forming in the walls and ceiling. Whenua pushed as hard as he could to increase the speed, then pushed a little harder, doing his best not to scream from the strain.

Suddenly, they were free. Both Toa dropped to the ground as the monstrous claw retreated back into the darkness. Nuju slammed the door after it and created a new lock of thick ice. Then he turned to Whenua, who was slowly powering down his drills.

"Ow," said the Toa of Ice.

"Sorry. All that I could think of," Whenua

replied. "No one is quite sure what that thing is, possibly a hybrid of an Ussal crab and some larger creature. But we do know it's practically blind and uses its hearing to track prey."

"Sensitive ears," said Nuju. "You gave it a headache."

Whenua stood and helped Nuju to his feet. "Welcome to the Archives."

"We're lost-wandering," said Orkahm. The Le-Matoran looked fearfully around at the unfamiliar sights of Ga-Metru. "We're never going to find that Great Disk!"

Vhisola gave him a hard look. "We're not lost," the Ga-Matoran snapped. "Just a little . . . turned around."

"You said you knew where we were ground-walking."

"I do!" Vhisola insisted. "It's around here, somewhere."

"Enough," Nokama, Toa Metru of Water, said sternly. "Arguing won't get us to the Great Disk any faster. It might even make things worse, Vhisola," she added, pointing down the avenue.

The Ga-Matoran turned to look. Then she gasped and took a step backwards. Standing beside one of the canals up ahead were three other

Ga-Matoran, all of them watching the approaching group with suspicion. One of them whispered to another, who then ran off toward the Great Temple.

Matau, Toa Metru of Air, watched the Ga-Matoran disappear and said, "So? They are curious-watching. What is the worry?"

Nokama dropped her voice to a whisper. "It's more than that. Those Matoran have been claimed by the Bordakh, the Ga-Metru Vahki squad. One touch of a Bordakh staff and a Matoran becomes so dedicated to order that he will turn in his best friend to preserve it."

"Spies," Matau replied. "Then I have a thought-plan. If it works, then we meet at the spillway quick-soon. Understand?"

"Yes, but what — ?"

"Ha! What do you know about Great Disks?" Matau boomed loud enough for the whole street to hear. "I will track-find the disk before you three can even check one proto-dam." Then the Toa of Air swung up into a chute and was gone.

The two Matoran down the road seemed to think about it for a moment, then they dashed off in the direction Matau had gone. Once Nokama was sure they were well away, she started running, dragging Vhisola and Orkahm behind her.

"Hey! Stop it!" Vhisola cried.

"They will not be able find him, and once they realize that, they will come back here. We must be elsewhere."

The Toa Metru of Water led them on a winding path through alleys, behind schools, over walls and finally to the site of one of Ga-Metru's mini-dams. Here tides of protodermis were held back so as not to overflow the metru's canal system. Nokama scanned the area but saw no sign of any Vahki or watchful Matoran. But she did see Matau standing in the middle of the spillway, arms folded across his chest and smiling.

"What took you so long?" he laughed.

"You stay here," Nokama said to Vhisola and Orkahm. "Keep an eye out for Bordakh."

Before either could argue, she ran, jumped,

flipped in mid-air and landed beside Matau. They were standing in a wide stone channel through which liquid protodermis flowed into the canals as needed. Right now, it was bone dry and would stay that way as long as the main valve was closed.

"You lost them?" she asked.

"No one catches a Toa-hero," Matau answered, leaning in close. "Unless, of course, he wants to be caught."

"Provided anyone wants to catch him," Nokama replied. "If we let a little protodermis out, we can swim through some of the lesser canals right to the Great Temple. Vhisola says we will find the disk there."

"Swim?" Matau said, with obvious disgust. "A Toa of Air doesn't swim — he high-flies."

"If he wants to get spotted by the Vahki, he does, yes. Turn the valve, just a little, and get some protodermis running through here. I will get the Matoran."

Shrugging, Matau walked over to the large wheel that controlled the valve. Then he stopped.

"Nokama? This is already open-wide." He grabbed the wheel and tried to turn it, but it would not move. "And locked!"

"What?" Nokama shouted, rushing toward him. She could already hear the roar of a proto-dermis wave heading for the spillway. "Matau, get out of here! Get —"

The wave smashed into the Toa of Water, sending her tumbling end over end. An instant later, Matau, too, was swept up in the flood. Not having Nokama's experience as a swimmer, he had not thought to grab a breath. Now he floundered, hand to his throat as the liquid protodermis filled his mouth and lungs.

Nokama extended her hydro blades in front of her and knifed through the protodermis. She slammed into Matau, her momentum carrying them both up toward the lip of the spillway. Then they were out of the liquid, landing hard on the stone ledge.

She rolled the Toa of Air over. "Matau? Matau!" she cried.

Matau choked and gasped. Then his eyes

snapped open and he looked at Nokama, a smile spreading across his face. "I knew you cared."

Nokama, Matau, Vhisola, and Orkahm walked hurriedly toward the Great Temple. There was no way to reach it without being seen, but they did their best to stay inconspicuous. For two Toa Metru, it wasn't easy. Matoran looked at them with wonder and awe, sometimes even fear, but none seemed hostile.

"'In Ga-Metru, go beyond the depths of Toa before,'" said Nokama. "That's what the carving said."

"And what does that scratch-writing mean?" asked Matau.

"In the sea, below the Great Temple," answered Vhisola. "Far below."

"Oh. Happy-cheer," said Matau, not sounding happy at all.

They circled around behind the Great Temple. Only a narrow stone walkway separated the building from the sea. Nokama had already announced that she would be going down alone to retrieve the disk.

"You and Orkahm are not swimmers," she told Matau. "But if something goes wrong, if I don't return, you will need Vhisola to show you the way out. So she stays here."

Matau was going to argue that Toa-heroes should work together. But the memory of almost drowning in protodermis was enough to keep him quiet. "Go quick-fast then, Toa Nokama. We will be waiting."

Nokama nodded, then dove into the turbulent sea of protodermis and vanished beneath the waves. Toa and Matoran stared after her, wondering what she might be encountering far below.

So caught up were they that they never heard the approach of others until it was too late. Matau glanced to the left and saw to his surprise three Bordakh, staffs at the ready, closing in. Three more moved toward them from the right, leaving their only escape the cold sea.

"I hate Ga-Metru," he muttered.

*   *   *

Nokama was unaware of what was going on up above. She had reached the very foundation of the Great Temple and spotted her prize. Wedged between two jagged outcroppings up ahead was a Great Disk!

The sight gave her renewed energy. She dove deeper and used all her new Toa strength to pry the disk loose. She checked the three-digit code and confirmed that, yes, this disk had been made in Ga-Metru and had a power level of 9. Only Great Disks possessed so much raw energy.

Smiling, she tucked it under her arm and started for the surface. She never noticed that those two jagged outcroppings had been massive teeth, or that their owner objected to her intrusion. She kicked her legs and swam, even as a pair of massive jaws prepared to snap shut upon her.

4

The first thing Onewa felt was the heat. It was never this hot in Po-Metru, not even in a Sculpture Field in the middle of the day. What in the name of Mata Nui was going on?

That's when he opened his eyes and saw the flames leaping in the furnace. Suddenly, he remembered the blast, the fall, everything. He shook Vakama, saying, "Wake up! Might be your last chance!"

The Toa of Fire's eyes snapped open and he looked around. They had moved a long way through the chute and were almost in the mouth of the furnace. There was no time to jump out of the chute, and once inside the melting chamber, not even the power of the Toa would save them.

"Don't you have a disk for this?" asked Onewa.

"Quiet! I have to concentrate," Vakama answered. He reached out his hands toward the mouth of the furnace and struggled to call upon his Toa energies. He knew that he had the ability to create fire. Now he was gambling that he could control it as well.

The chute brought them closer and closer to the end. Onewa wondered if his Mask of Power might be able to rescue them, then sadly remembered that he did not even know what power his mask possessed. It was up to Vakama.

The Toa of Fire summoned every last bit of his willpower and hurled it at the furnace. Then, to his amazement, the fires began to flicker. He felt heat pouring into his body as the flames died down to mere sparks. Soon, even the sparks were gone.

"I don't believe it," Onewa whispered. "How did you — ?"

"Watch out!" Vakama yelled, just before unleashing twin white-hot bursts of flame that burned a hole through the ceiling of the building. The streams of fire lasted for a long, long moment before Vakama cut them off. Then he finally collapsed, exhausted.

"What did you do?"

"Absorbed the fire," said Vakama, out of breath. "But I couldn't contain the power. Had to release it, or . . ."

Onewa glanced up in time to see Nidhiki back away from the railing and vanish into the darkness. He considered giving chase, but he knew his four-legged enemy would already be long gone. Besides, there was a worse problem to be faced.

"That fire blast, Vakama, it's going to bring the Vahki on the run," he said, helping the Toa of Fire to his feet. "The Nuurakh will haul us in for destruction of metru property and our mission will be over."

"Nuhrii and Ahkmou?"

Onewa shook his head. "My guess is we're going to have to find them. Again. Let's go."

As it turned out, tracking down the two Matoran was not very difficult. Ahkmou had been to Ta-

Metru before, but didn't know it well, and wasn't willing to risk running into Nidhiki. Nuhrii did know all the alleyways and shortcuts, but was too frightened to go very far. Onewa found them hiding among some chutes that were closed for repair.

Vakama knelt down and looked at both of them. "Listen to me. It should be obvious now that someone doesn't want us to find the Great Disks. That means neither one of you is safe until they *are* found. Understand?"

Nuhrii nodded. Ahkmou shrugged. Vakama decided that would have to be enough.

"Then let's go to the fire pits."

The Ta-Metru fire pits consisted of a half dozen deep, narrow craters from which spewed forth great jets of flame. A nest of underground pipelines fed the fires to wherever they were needed in the metru. Given their importance, it was no surprise that the site was fenced in and guarded by Nuurakh.

"Can't we just go up and tell them why we need the disk?" asked Nuhrii.

"If they listened, and if they believed us, and if they were willing to take us to Turaga Dume to explain, maybe we would get the disk," said Onewa. "Or maybe not. So we bend the rules. Hey, you can't make a sculpture without shattering some protodermis, right?"

"We need a distraction," said Vakama.

Onewa smiled. "Done."

A few moments later, they were in position. Vakama and Nuhrii had crept as close to the fence as they could without being seen. Onewa and Ahkmou had moved near a pile of stone left over from a recent excavation.

At Vakama's signal, Onewa focused his elemental power. First, one block of stone went flying to crash against the fence. Then two, then six, until the Vahki rushed over to see what was happening. Onewa got a little carried away and sent a block crashing into one of the Nuurakh.

As soon as the Vahki had left their posts, Vakama and Nuhrii rushed forward. Vakama used his power to heat up the fence and melt a hole for the two of them. "Are you sure you know which fire pit contains the disk?" the Toa Metru whispered.

"I saw a carving," answered Nuhrii. "I think it was correct."

The Matoran led Vakama to the lip of one of the pits. The Toa of Fire peered over, then jumped back as the flames roared from it. Once the fires subsided, he said, "Come on, we don't have long!"

Melting handholds in the sides of the pit, Vakama climbed down with Nuhrii clinging to him. Down below, he could see a disk wedged into the wall, somehow intact despite the intense heat. Vakama reached down and pried it loose. Yes, it did have the symbol of Ta-Metru on it, and its three-digit disk code indicated it had a power level of 9 — the highest known concentration of energy possible in a Kanoka disk.

This was a Great Disk!

"We have it," said Vakama. "Climb over me and get out of the pit."

Nuhrii clambered over Vakama's shoulders, but before he could make it to the surface, twin Morbuzakh vines shot up from the depths below. They wrapped themselves tightly around Toa and Matoran and began to drag them down into the fire pit.

"Free yourself and get out of here! Get the Great Disk to Onewa!" Vakama shouted.

"I can't, it's too strong! We're Vahki bones!" Nuhrii answered, frantic. "The fire pit will erupt any moment!"

The Toa of Fire redoubled his efforts but the more he struggled, the harder the vine pulled. Worse, he was bound in such a way that there was no room in the pit for him to aim and launch a disk.

"Nuhrii, can you reach my last disk? I need you to load it in the launcher."

The Matoran nodded and strained to reach the disk. He could just barely brush his fingertips against it. "I can't reach!"

"Try! It's more than just us — the whole city is at stake," said Vakama.

Nuhrii stretched until the pain was so great he could barely think straight. But his hand closed around the disk. "It's a power level 4," he reported. "Power code 1."

As Nuhrii fitted the disk in the launcher, Vakama continued to fight to get free. Power code 1 was able to reconstitute whatever it touched at random. It was a dangerous disk to use because it was just as apt to make the Morbuzakh more powerful than less. But they had no choice.

Nuhrii wrestled against the might of the Morbuzakh to get the launcher into the right position. When it was as well-aimed as he could manage, he triggered the mechanism and launched the disk at the spot where the two vines joined.

It struck the target head-on. Vakama watched, amazed, as the molecules that made up the vines were scrambled. The shock made the plant loosen its grip. The Toa of Fire and Nuhrii scrambled out of the pit.

Vakama caught a flash of the new form of the Morbuzakh — a thick vine with long, sharp thorns and what looked like a mouth lined with razor-sharp teeth. It gave out an eerie howl and tried to reach Vakama, just as the pit exploded into flames again. The Toa Metru knew the flames would not destroy the vine, but he had no wish to wait around and see that horror again.

Toa and Matoran ran for the fence. Both made a point of not looking behind them.

5

"What about this one?" asked Nuju, pointing to a metallic door that looked thick and solid.

Whenua turned, looked, and shook his head. "No. It's not behind that one."

"How do you know?"

"Because I know what's in there. Leave it alone."

Nuju glared at the Toa of Earth. Back in Ko-Metru, Nuju had been an important scholar with vital responsibilities. Now he was a Toa Metru, reduced to tramping around dark, musty Archives looking for one relic among thousands. So far, he had been squeezed in an Ussal crab claw, weakened by a frost leech, stepped in something whose origin he really did not want to know, and gotten hopelessly lost at least twice. He was covered in the dust of the past and he did not like it.

"Whenua doesn't seem to have any idea

what is down here," Nuju muttered to himself. "So how does he know the Great Disk isn't behind this door?"

Checking to make sure the Toa of Earth was otherwise occupied, Nuju grasped the handle of the door and pulled. Surprisingly, it wasn't locked. It took his eyes a moment to adjust to the even deeper darkness behind the door. Once they had, he noticed something that seemed to be shimmering. Could the Great Disk create an effect like that?

He took a step inside, then another, before his progress was stopped by a clear wall. No, it wasn't a wall. It was the side of a tank filled with liquid protodermis. He pressed his mask against the glass, trying to see what, if anything, was in there.

Suddenly something slammed hard against the inside of the tank, right where Nuju was standing. Before the Toa could react, it had circled and smashed into the tank wall again, this time creating a hairline crack. On its third pass, Nuju got a good look at it, and wished he hadn't.

The creature was long, serpent-like, with powerful forearms and, most disturbing, two heads. Both heads featured narrow greenish eyes and a fanged mouth.

Nuju jumped back as it struck again. Now protodermis was starting to leak from the tank, but this was something he could handle. A minimal amount of his power was enough to freeze it and seal the crack. But his presence had obviously disturbed the creature, so he felt that he had better leave.

He turned around. Whenua was standing in the doorway, watching him.

"Done?" asked the Toa of Earth. "Listen, I know you don't like it here. It's not neat and orderly like Ko-Metru. Archivists don't sit in clean towers studying all day, they are out getting their hands dirty. But we have rules here too — like don't annoy the two-headed Tarakava, if at all possible."

Nuju nodded. "It does seem . . . excitable."

"Last ones to excite it before it came here were two Ga-Matoran in a fishing skiff," Whenua said, turning and walking away. "They were lucky to make it out of the sea. The skiff wound up as sawdust."

Nuju said nothing. He followed behind Whenua, reminding himself that even in a place devoted to the dead past, actions could have consequences.

Whenua stopped at another doorway. His expression was troubled. "It could be in here. It probably would be in here, the way things are going. But, by Mata Nui, I hope it's not."

This door actually had a sign, which read "Keep out." Nuju wondered what could be behind there that would worry Whenua so much. After all, two Toa Metru should be able to handle anything.

Whenua hesitated before using his earth-shock drill to punch through the lock. "I hope we're ready for this. The last archivist that came down here hasn't spoken a word since. Screams a lot, though."

Nuju readied both of his crystal spikes, in case his ice power would be needed. Whenua slowly opened the door and the two of them stepped inside.

They found themselves in a large, brightly lit room. It was completely bare. There was no sign that any creature lived there, or ever had lived there. Nuju frowned. *This didn't look very frightening at all. What had Whenua been so worried about?*

Both Toa Metru whirled at the sound of the door slamming behind them. Even more surprising, Nuju could see the hole made by Whenua's drills disappearing. They were locked in.

"What is this?" asked Nuju.

"No one knows exactly," said Whenua, looking all around. "Our best theory is that this creature has some connection to the random reconstitution disk power."

"*What* creature? There's nothing here!" said Nuju.

"You don't understand," Whenua replied, as the lightstones suddenly began to dim. "This Rahi isn't in the room. It *is* the room!"

The floor beneath Nuju's feet began to

shift. A pair of clawed hands emerged from the stone to grasp him around the ankles. A much larger hand sprang forth from one of the walls and narrowly missed grabbing Whenua. The room echoed with a low, ominous rumble that sounded like the breathing of a massive creature.

The Toa of Earth dove toward where Nuju stood. Spikes shot out of the walls just above him, but Whenua was too nimble to be caught. He grabbed the two hands holding Nuju and wrenched them free. The roar in the room grew louder and angrier.

Now the floor was rising fast, sending both Toa toward a crushing end against the ceiling. Nuju fired streams of ice from his crystal spikes, forming thick pillars to keep floor and ceiling apart. But he knew they would not hold for long.

"We have to get out of here," he said.

"Any ideas?" asked Whenua.

"I was hoping you had one."

Whenua smiled. "Maybe I do. You can do ice, but what else can you do?"

Nuju needed no more prompting. He gathered his energies and concentrated on conjuring a storm. It was incredibly hard, unskilled as he still was in the use of his elemental powers. But little by little the air began to turn colder, and a chill wind started to blow through the confines of the room. Moisture in the air condensed into droplets, which then froze into crystals of snow.

Nuju strained to lower the temperature more, and then still more. Beside him, Whenua shivered, frost forming on his mask. It was an open question who would succumb to the storm first, the Toa Metru or the creature that had trapped them.

Then Whenua was pointing to something on the far wall. Nuju strained to see through the snow and ice. It looked like an opening in the wall. As the two Toa moved toward it, a wave passed through the floor beneath them, hurling them toward the gap. They flew out of the room and crashed against the wall of the hallway. Behind them, the gap closed again.

Whenua groaned and brushed the ice off his body. "I guess it worked. This hasn't been as easy as I thought it would be."

"Maybe that's the first lesson in the life of a Toa," replied Nuju. "Nothing is easy."

The Toa of Ice was starting to feel he was walking in circles. This sub-level of the Archives seemed to go on forever, and he felt certain they had seen some of these doors before. But Whenua insisted that wasn't so.

"If it's here, we will have to find it soon," the Toa of Earth insisted. "We have explored almost the entire level. I don't think —"

He stopped abruptly and cocked his head, listening to something. Now Nuju could hear it too — the steady tramp of feet from somewhere in the halls. The footsteps were too heavy to be Matoran, and anyway archivists avoided this section.

Whenua glanced at Nuju. "We just ran out of time. The Vahki are coming. Someone must have heard all the noise down here and called for them."

The Toa of Earth started frantically opening doors. "We're down here without authorization, planning to take an artifact. Never mind that it's in a good cause. You know the Onu-Metru Vahki. The Rorzakh will chase us through this entire place and all the way back to the Great Temple before they give up!"

Nuju had to admit he was right. Even in Ko-Metru, Matoran knew never to get a Rorzakh on their trail. There was no risk they wouldn't take to get their job done. There was even a story that a Rorzakh had once plunged into a mine shaft, in free fall, to try and catch a lawbreaker.

The Toa of Ice started pulling open doors on the run. "I never imagined being a Toa would involve searching for so many things. I thought Toa had everything they needed."

"Maybe not," said Whenua. "Maybe Toa are just the only ones who have the power to find what has to be found."

The Toa of Earth yanked another door open. An avalanche of Metru Nui artifacts tumbled out, knocking him off his feet and burying him beneath a pile of tools, masks, stone tablets, and more.

For a moment, all was silent. Nuju took a step toward the pile when the artifacts started to shift. Then Whenua's hand shot out of the pile, holding the Great Disk.

Nuju smiled. It was time to gather the two Matoran and head to Ko-Metru where, he was certain, the search for the Great Disk would proceed in a much more orderly way.

Nokama swam in long, steady strokes, her eyes focused on the surface. She could make out indistinct figures through the water. There was Matau, and Vhisola, Orkahm, and . . . Vahki!

The sight made her stop short. Only then did she sense the disturbance in the water, as if nature itself were crying out to her. She whirled to see the giant sea beast closing in on her. She wanted to scream, but opening her mouth underwater would save the Rahi the trouble of ending her existence.

Nokama forced her fear away. It was all right for a Matoran to be afraid, but she was a Toa now. She could fight back, and just maybe solve two problems at once.

Clutching the Great Disk tightly, she sped for the surface. The monstrous Rahi was right on top of her, caught up in the hunt and determined to catch a meal. Nokama burst out of the water and into the air, diving toward one group of Vahki. The beast followed close behind, leaping, jaws snapping, hungry for its prey.

At the last possible moment, Nokama curled into a ball and flipped downwards. Unable to change direction, the Rahi slammed into the startled Vahki. Matau used the distraction to summon a strong wind and blow the other Vahki into the water.

"Now we are in trouble-danger," said Matau. "Vahki hate fish. And baths."

"Then let's not wait for their complaints," said Nokama. "We have the disk. Let's go!"

The four did not stop running until they had reached the borders of Le-Metru. Here they lost themselves in the crowds that filled the transport hub of Metru Nui. Vhisola kept looking over her shoulder as if she expected the Vahki to be gaining.

"Why am I here?" she asked. "You have the

Ga-Metru disk. I don't know anything about the Le-Metru disk! Why can't I go home?"

"You are safer with us," said Nokama.

"Yes, four-legged Rahi-breath out there somewhere," added Matau. "You wouldn't want to run into him."

Neither Toa Metru chose to tell the whole story. Each of the six Matoran who had joined the Toa on their quest for the disks had their own reasons for wanting the artifacts. For some, it was personal glory, for some spite, and the heroes believed Ahkmou wanted the disks for far darker reasons. Both Nokama and Matau felt letting either of their Matoran wander off was risking more trouble with the Vahki, or worse.

Matau led them to a strangely quiet section of the metru, marked by broken chutes and mangled support beams. No repair crews were in sight, nor any chute operators. Nokama glanced at Matau, who said simply, "Morbuzakh."

The Toa of Water looked around, concerned. An area of the metru ravaged by Morbuzakh vines would make a good hiding place, but it also meant the plant might strike here again. They would have to be on their guard.

"What did the carving-speak say about the Le-Metru disk?" Matau asked.

"The Great Disk of Le-Metru will be all around you when you find it," answered Nokama.

Matau looked left and right. "I don't see it."

"That's because it's not here," said Orkahm. "You won't find it by moving fast, Matau. As hard as it might be for you, you will have to slow down to retrieve it."

Matau frowned. To a high-flying Toa Metru like him, "slow down" sounded like a curse. "So where is it hidden-lost?"

"That's just it," said Orkahm. "I found it, but it's not in that place anymore. It could be any-where by now. It's in a force sphere!"

Matau sat down heavily, his eyes on the ground. Nokama looked from him to Orkahm and back again. "Is that bad?" she asked.

"Very," Matau replied, nodding. "Very, very."

"Is someone going to explain to me what's going on, or do you need a downpour to convince you?" she snapped.

"All right, you know what a chute is?" said Orkahm. "It's protodermis with a magnetic energy sheath that keeps things fast-moving through it. Sometimes, if there's a break-flaw in the chute construction, some of that energy snaps off and wraps-folds in on itself."

"It travels everquick through the chutes," said Matau. "Its magnetism draws things inside: tools, debris . . . and a Great Disk. The longer it exists, the more mighty-strong it becomes."

"And then what happens?" asked Nokama, not sure she wanted to hear the answer.

"When it gets big enough and strong enough, it rips-tears chutes to pieces," said the Toa of Air. "Force sphere gets deep-buried under the wreckage and implodes. All gone."

"Along with everything inside it," said Nokama grimly. "We have to find it!"

Orkahm pulled out a chute map of Le-

Metru and showed it to the two Toa, pointing to one junction close by. "It was here just before Toa Matau and I high-flew to the Great Temple."

Toa Matau traced the force sphere's most likely route until he came to a spot on the map that looked to Nokama like a complete tangle of chutes. "There! Too many chutes wrapped around each other will slow it down. We'll find it there!"

"There" turned out to be an ancient portion of the metru, apparently built long before anyone tried making sense of the chute system. Nokama had never seen anything quite so complex or scrambled together. She wondered how any Matoran made it through what Matau called "the Notch."

The Toa of Air was perched up above one of the chutes, his keen eyes scanning the route. If he was right, the force sphere would come flying by any moment. All he would have to do would be jump inside it, grab the Great Disk, and then get back out.

"Easy!" he insisted. "Except for the getting

out. And the getting in. And maybe seek-finding the disk."

Orkahm cried out. The force sphere was barreling through the chute, heading for the Notch at an incredible rate of speed. It was larger than a Toa and its interior was a whirlpool of magnetic energy and protodermis fragments. Nokama questioned whether anything living could survive in there.

If Matau was worried, he didn't show it. As the sphere passed through the chute beneath him, he dove inside.

Instantly, the energies of the sphere took hold of him, threatening to tear him to pieces. Tools, bolts, and other small items swirled about him in a mad dance, striking him again and again. Meanwhile, the sphere continued on its rapid pace toward the Notch.

Outside, Orkahm's eyes widened. He and Matau had been wrong. The sphere was not going to slow down for the Notch! It was going to rip it to pieces and then collapse in on itself, taking the Toa of Air and the Great Disk with it.

Matau could sense what was happening, but it was too late to do anything about it. If he jumped out now, he would lose the Great Disk and the city would be doomed. If he stayed, at least there was a slim chance he could —

Yes! Reaching out blindly, he had grasped something that felt like a disk. Fighting the pull of the sphere, he brought it close enough to his mask to see it was indeed the Le-Metru Great Disk. As he admired it, a chunk of protodermis smashed into his hand, almost making him lose his grip.

Matau couldn't see out of the sphere, but he knew the Notch had to be coming up fast. He had to overcome the sphere's pull and leap out now, but there was nothing to brace himself against. Without that, he could do nothing but tumble helplessly like all the rest of the sphere's captive debris.

My own strength will not be enough, he told himself. *I will have to match my Toa-power against it.*

The last time Matau had used his elemental abilities, it had taken all his concentration to form just a simple cushion of air. This time, it seemed to come a little easier, but he was also attempting a much harder task. It was going to take a mini-cyclone to overcome the force sphere's power and tear himself free.

There was no time to let the winds build up slowly. Matau pushed his powers to their limit, forcing the air around him to swirl violently. Suddenly, he was in the center of a whirlwind which sucked the breath from his lungs. It was an open question whether the implosion would end his existence or suffocation would do it first.

The world became a blur as Matau spun around and around inside the cyclone. He could feel himself beginning to black out, but knew if he did, the windstorm would cease and any hope of escaping the sphere would be gone. He fought to stay conscious. After all, it wouldn't look very impressive to Nokama if the Toa of Air perished on his first big mission.

Then suddenly he was flying through the air. It took him an instant to realize he had been thrown free of the force sphere. Unfortunately, his whirlwind was still active, sending him hurling into a support post with a loud crash.

Nokama, Vhisola, and Orkahm ran over to where Matau lay on the ground. The Toa of Air wasn't moving. Hesitantly, Nokama reached out and touched his shoulder. "Matau?"

He rolled over abruptly and, smiling, thrust up a hand holding the Great Disk. "See, Nokama?" he said. "I told you, no worry-problem!"

7

In Metru Nui, Ko-Matoran were known for many things. Their devotion to learning was second to none. Their ambition to become Knowledge Tower scholars was incredibly powerful. Their attitude toward Matoran from other metru was usually cold, and sometimes bordered on rude. Since they almost always had their attention focused on a tablet, a carving, or some complicated philosophical problem, they often missed things going on around them.

That was why none of the Ko-Matoran bothered to look up and notice Toa Metru Whenua hanging on to a tower for dear life.

"I thought you were good at this," Nuju snapped, scrambling to pull his fellow Toa back onto the roof.

"No, that's Onewa who swings around

buildings," shouted Whenua. "I'm Whenua, who falls off them!"

With a mighty heave, Nuju succeeded in yanking the Toa of Earth back to relative safety on top of the ice-covered Knowledge Tower. Whenua immediately used his earthshock drills to dig himself handholds.

"Don't damage the crystal underneath," warned Nuju. "I should have gone with my first instinct and done this by myself. I knew what the consequences of this alliance would be."

"We worked together all right in Onu-Metru. Remember? Oh, I forgot, you ignore the past, don't you?" Whenua replied. "Besides, if you worked alone, you would probably just wind up like poor Tehutti."

The Onu-Matoran was standing on a nearby rooftop with Ehrye, his eyes wide and confused. Ehrye had a grip on his arm to keep him from wandering off. The four of them had encountered a patrol of Keerakh, the Ko-Metru Vahki, and Tehutti had made the mistake of running. One swipe of a Keerakh staff and he lost all sense of time and place. Judging by the things he had said since, Tehutti thought he was back in the Archives cataloging a Fikou spider exhibit.

"Are you sure the Great Disk is up here?" Whenua asked, getting cautiously to his feet. The winds were strong this high up and the Knowledge Tower rooftops had steep inclines. One slip and down he would tumble again.

"You were there when Nokama translated the carving," replied Nuju. "In Ko-Metru, find where the sky and ice are joined. Besides, Ehrye says it is near here, atop one of these Knowledge Towers."

Nuju stood at the edge of the roof and studied the gap between this tower and the next. His first attempt to travel by ice slide had failed miserably, so he was reluctant to do it again. Better to leap and rely on his crystal spikes to stop any fall.

Taking a running start, Nuju jumped into space. He had gauged his leap perfectly, arcing down close enough to the next tower that he could catch the side with a spike and anchor himself. Back on the other roof, Whenua looked on, frustrated.

Nuju raised his free spike and fired a blast of ice. When he was done, there was a thick, frozen beam in place between the two towers. "Wrap your arms around it and slide across," he instructed Whenua.

The Toa of Earth did some quick calculations, which included his new mass post-transformation, the thickness of the ice, and the velocity he would achieve just before he was smashed flat on the ground below. When he was done, he reported, "It will never hold."

"Yes, it will," Nuju insisted. "Probably," he added quietly.

Whenua jumped, caught the ice beam, and rapidly slid across the gap. He had made it halfway when the ice began to crack and splinter behind him. He struck the side of the building and dug in his earthshock drills even as the beam collapsed completely.

"Ko-Metru needs more chutes," Whenua muttered.

"Most Ko-Matoran don't travel by rooftop," said Nuju. "Look below."

Looking down was not high on Whenua's list of things to do, but the urgency in Nuju's voice left no room for argument. The Ko-Matoran far below looked like microscopic organisms, but those weren't what Nuju was pointing out. No, it was the half dozen Keerakh scuttling through the crowd and heading right for this particular Knowledge Tower that had the Toa of Ice worried.

"I thought we had left them far behind," said Whenua.

"Keerakh are efficient," answered Nuju. "We are not where we're supposed to be. It's their job to change that. Keep moving."

The two Toa Metru made it to the top of the tower. Whenua looked over the side and saw the Keerakh were climbing up the side of the building. "We have problems, Nuju."

"Worse than you know," said Nuju, pointing to the next tower. Three more of the Ko-Metru Vahki were gathered on its roof, waiting.

"Keerakh have found a way to take the element of chance out of tracking. They simply figure out where you are going and get there first."

"Have a plan?"

"Something like that," said Nuju, levelling his crystal spike and sending a blast of ice at Whenua. Instantly, the Toa of Earth was covered in a thick layer of ice from shoulders to knees.

"What are you doing?" Whenua demanded, struggling in vain to get free.

Nuju ignored him and turned to the Vahki on the opposite roof. "After a long pursuit, I have caught this thief from Onu-Metru. Take him to Turaga Dume for punishment."

The three Vahki looked at each other, obviously trying to figure out when the strange being with the twin spikes joined their side. With the closest thing Keerakh could give to a shrug, they sprang from their perch to take custody of Whenua.

In mid-leap, Nuju caught them with an ice blast and froze them solid. One swipe of his spike shattered the ice surrounding Whenua. "The

Vahki have kindly provided us with a bridge. Let's use it."

The two Toa Metru ran across the bridge of frozen Keerakh to the next roof. Nuju looked over his shoulder to make sure Ehrye and Tehutti were well-hidden a few towers back, then turned his attention to Whenua. "Are you all right?"

"Well, I won't be in a hurry to visit the icier parts of the Archives for a while," the Toa of Earth replied. "Next time, give me a little warning."

"All right. Hit the ground," said Nuju as he dove flat on the roof. Whenua joined him just as Nuju used his spikes to create a thin layer of snow and ice over them both. "Keep quiet," the Toa of Ice whispered.

Whenua could barely make out what was going on outside their icy shell. He spotted the shapes of the Keerakh reaching the top of the other roof. Half of them immediately went to work chipping away at the ice bridge while the other half crossed it in pursuit. One walked right over where the Toa lay, camouflaged.

Whenua started to rise. Nuju grabbed his arm and said softly, "Not yet. Wait."

"Wait? Wait for what?"

"You're the archivist," Nuju said quietly. "What do you know about Keerakh?"

"Let's see. Ko-Metru Vahki. Order enforcement technique is disorientation. Hard to hide from because they're always one . . . step . . . ahead of . . ." Whenua smiled.

"Exactly," said Nuju. "I do not know how they do it, but they do. So rather than run from them —"

"We follow them," Whenua finished. "And they lead us right to the Great Disk."

Of course, following Vahki was easier said than done. In their dormant state, Vahki occupied a circular hive, with one Vahki monitoring each direction. Though they appeared to be completely inactive, Vahki sensory apparatus never fully shut down. Any sound or movement was instantly detected. When Vahki traveled, they moved in much the same way, always with an eye turned toward the flanks and rear.

For that reason, Nuju had recommended that Ehrye and Tehutti be left behind. Tehutti kept ranting about misfiled Fikou anyway, and Ehrye was in no hurry to walk into a possible Keerakh trap. So the two Toa Metru traveled alone, relying on speed and stealth to keep up with the Vahki and keep out of sight.

Their journey ended at a central tower. The half dozen Vahki paused there and began to mill around. After a few moments, each Keerakh locked its four legs into place on the icy roof and settled in to wait.

Nuju frowned. "Of course, there is one problem with this plan."

"That's a change — you not thinking ahead," said Whenua. "Maybe what the Vahki need is a little disorder. Get me down from up here."

Nuju moved to the far edge of the rooftop and checked to make sure the Vahki had not yet noticed their presence. Then he used his elemental energies to create a thick pole of ice stretching from the roof to the avenue below.

"I was thinking more like pointing me toward a chute," said Whenua.

"This is faster."

"Right. At least it will be over quick," said Whenua, getting ready to ride down the pole. "When you see your opportunity, get that disk. I'll meet you in Ga-Metru."

Nuju watched as the Toa of Earth slid down and vanished in the icy mist. Then he went back to watching the Vahki.

Down below, Whenua was doing his best not to get sick. He was moving much too fast, with no way to slow down. At this rate, he would succeed in distracting the Vahki by making a very large hole in the street.

On the rooftop above, Nuju was counting quietly to himself. When he reached 10, he launched two more bursts of ice from his crystal spikes. They arced over the side of the building and disappeared.

Whenua saw the ice bolts approach and then pass him. The next thing he knew, he was flying down a winding ice slide that had suddenly formed around the pole. The angle of the slide kept changing so that, little by little, Whenua's descent was slowed. He still hit the ground hard, but Nuju's calculations were correct. The Toa of Earth hadn't suffered any serious injury.

That's the second time he's surprised me today, thought Whenua. *Hope it isn't going to become a habit.*

He looked around. A few Ko-Matoran had looked up from their studies long enough to notice that a Toa Metru had just dropped into their midst. It was only a matter of time before one summoned additional Vahki. Whenua went to work, using his earthshock drills to cut a hole in the street.

Once the opening was wide enough, the

Toa dropped down. As an archivist, he knew the underground of Metru Nui better than any of the other Toa. Immediately beneath the streets were mechanisms designed to help keep the metru clean, protodermis pipes, and the occasional nest of rodent Rahi. Farther down would be whatever sub-levels of the Archives had extended this far, and beneath that . . . beneath that, he preferred not to think about.

For now, he was only worried about the immediate sub-surface. Using one drill to bore through the street above, he used the other to disrupt the cleaning mechanisms, break the occasional narrow pipe, and generally make a mess. He made no effort to keep it quiet — the more noise the better.

He knew what would be happening above right now. Ko-Matoran would be looking around in wonder and annoyance at the disturbance. The sound would be traveling up to the sensitive ears of the Vahki. They would never be able to resist the chance to clamp down on such obvious disorder.

* * *

High above, the Vahki were proving Whenua right. First one, then two, peered over the side of the roof to see what was happening below. Unable to get a good look due to the icy mist that perpetually hovered over Ko-Metru, the Vahki squad left their positions and began climbing down the side of the Knowledge Tower.

Nuju waited until they were gone, then leapt to the next roof. He was sure the Great Disk must be there somewhere, but he saw no sign of it. He scrambled to get a little higher on the inclined roof and slipped, hurtling toward the edge.

Before he could put his crystal spikes to use, he had fallen over the side. At the last moment, he reached out and grabbed a huge icicle that hung from the ledge. It wasn't unusual to see icicles up this high, but he quickly noticed that this one was just a little different from the rest.

Frozen in its heart was a Great Disk.

Beneath the street, Whenua continued his labors, keeping an eye on the hole through which he had come. As soon as he saw Keerakh peering down through it, he knew it was time to be elsewhere. Revving up his drills, he punched a hole through the floor and then through the next level as well. Plunging through the gap, he tumbled into an Archives sub-level.

No Ko-Metru Vahki would ever find him down here. He took off at a run, following the winding corridors in the direction of Ga-Metru. If all had gone well, he would meet Nuju there with two Great Disks between them.

Toa Onewa and Ahkmou walked side by side through the Po-Metru sculpture fields, Vakama and Nurhii bringing up the rear. The journey had been made largely in silence, with the exception of Ahkmou giving directions to the hiding place of the Great Disk. They had already taken a few wrong turns thanks to the Matoran's "forgetting" exactly where it was concealed.

"It's not far," Ahkmou said.

"That's the tenth time you've said that," Onewa replied. "I'm beginning to think you don't want us to find the Great Disk."

"Of course I do," said Ahkmou. "Okay, so maybe I wanted them for myself at first. But now I realize that you six Toa need them to save the whole city. I wouldn't get in the way of that. Only, what are you going to do with the Great Disks once you have them?"

Onewa shrugged. "I don't know. This is Vakama's plan. I suppose we'll give them to him."

Ahkmou chuckled. "I see. So he gets all of you to go out and gather the six most powerful items in all of Metru Nui, and then you just turn them over to him? No questions asked? I wish I had thought of that."

I bet you do, thought Onewa darkly.

"So who's this four-legged friend of yours? The one who likes pushing Toa into furnaces?" asked the Toa of Stone.

"He's no friend," answered Ahkmou. "We were . . . business partners. He asked me to get him the Great Disks. Doing it seemed like a better idea than having him angry at me. He didn't say why he wanted them."

"And you didn't ask. What did he promise you in return?"

"Protection," said Ahkmou. "Something we both need right now. Look!"

Po-Matoran were running from the Sculpture Fields in a panic. Only two things had been known to make crafters move that fast: quitting time and a rogue tunneler. Unfortunately, it was too early for work to be done for the day.

Tunnelers had been a problem in Po-Metru for as long as Onewa could remember. They were lizard-like Rahi, normally about twice as long as Matoran were tall, with an appetite for solid protodermis. They had been known to dig up into warehouses and consume everything from raw protodermis blocks to finished tools. Rarely did they pose a real threat to the Matoran workers, but every now and then one went bad and began rampaging through the work areas.

Vakama and Nuhrii had caught up now. "What's going on?" asked the Toa of Fire.

"A little problem," said Onewa.

"A big problem," corrected Ahkmou.

The tunneler had emerged from beneath the surface into the middle of the Sculpture Field. It was bigger than any Onewa had ever seen, easily three times the size of a Toa. Worse, its scales were mottled with dark patches and its eyes were red. In a tunneler, both were sure signs of madness.

"Maybe I can scare it off," suggested Vakama. Before Onewa could stop him, he had lobbed a few small fireballs in the direction of the tunneler. Not wanting to hurt the beast, Vakama had aimed well over its head.

If the tunneler could have smiled, it would have. As the fireballs approached, it reared up on its hind legs and purposely let itself be hit. An instant later, it had transformed from a creature of scales and claws to a monster of flame.

"We're not in your metru, Vakama. Fire's not the answer to everything," Onewa said sharply. "Tunnelers absorb whatever power you throw at them. We've gone from a menace to a catastrophe."

All around the creature, sculptures had begun to melt. Every step it took left a charred footprint in the soil. Even at a great distance, the two Toa Metru could feel the heat.

"If that thing makes it out of the Sculpture Fields, all of Po-Metru could burn," said Onewa. "Let's see if it wants to play catch."

The Toa of Stone lifted a huge boulder and prepared to throw it. Vakama couldn't understand his strategy — most of the rock would melt before it ever reached the tunneler, and what was left wouldn't do any damage.

Onewa tossed the boulder. It began to glow and melt as it got closer to its target. But enough made it through that the tunneler had to bat the fragments away with its tail. As soon as rock met tunneler, the creature transformed again, this time becoming a thing of stone.

"Well, that helps a little," said Onewa. The tunneler brushed lightly against a massive sculpture, and the statue crumbled from the blow. "Or not."

"I have an idea, but we'll need Nuhrii and Ahkmou's help," said Vakama. He turned around and saw both Matoran were gone. A moment later, he heard the sounds of a struggle from behind one of the sculptures.

The Toa of Fire looked behind the statue. Nuhrii had Ahkmou pinned on the ground.

"He was trying to run away again," said the Ta-Matoran. "But he brought us here. Seems to me he should help us get out again."

"You're both going to help. Here's what we're going to do."

The tunneler slowly blinked its stone eyes. Two of the little ones were still in its sight, jumping and yelling in a language it didn't understand. The two larger ones had disappeared. Ordinarily, there was no cause to harm little ones, unless they got in the way of a meal. But these two were annoying with their noise.

With a snarl, the tunneler lumbered forward to silence them.

"Now!" shouted Onewa. He slung his proto piton onto a nearby statue and he and Vakama swung from their perch high above. As they passed over the tunneler, Vakama unleashed a quick, intense fire blast at the ground.

Fire met sand right in front of the creature,

fusing the ground into glass. Startled by the light and heat, the creature whipped its tail forward, striking the new glass surface. That was all it took for the tunneler of stone to change to a tunneler of crystal.

The creature spotted the two Toa Metru and started to take a step forward, only to be stopped by the sound of a sharp crack. Its new glass body wasn't strong enough to support the tunneler's size. Every move it made caused another hairline fracture to appear, so the tunneler wisely decided to stay still.

"That should keep it occupied until the Vahki arrive," said Onewa. "Then the archivists can decide what to do with it."

Onewa looked up at the tallest sculpture he had ever seen. It looked like an upside down mountain, balancing on its peak. Nokama had said that the Toa must seek a "mountain in balance" if they were to find the Po-Metru Great Disk. This certainly looked like the spot.

"It's up there," confirmed Ahkmou. "Embedded in a jagged hole near the top. Good luck getting it out."

The thought of the climb made even the Toa of Stone a little dizzy. He had no doubt he could get up there. It was getting down that might pose a problem.

"Are you sure you want to go up there alone?" asked Vakama. "I could —"

"No," Onewa replied. "If I have to be concerned about me falling, I don't want to have to be worrying about you falling too. Besides, if I don't make it down . . ."

Vakama nodded. Risking both Toa Metru would be foolish. Someone had to be left to get the Great Disk if Onewa failed.

The Toa of Stone dug one of his proto pitons into the side of the sculpture and began to climb. Vakama, Ahkmou, and Nuhrii watched him as he slowly ascended, each alone with his thoughts.

Onewa moved slowly, but steadily. His new body was far stronger than his Matoran form had been, but still his shoulders and arms already ached from the effort. And there was still so far to go.

His thoughts drifted back to the Great Temple and the moment he and the others had become Toa. He had certainly never imagined, when he brought the Toa stone there, that his whole life was about to change. Nor would he necessarily have picked his five fellow heroes of Metru Nui. Vakama was too much of a dreamer, Nokama seemed a little stuck on herself, Matau was simply annoying, and Nuju and Whenua argued constantly.

Still, they must have been chosen for this honor for a reason. Just as a Po-Metru crafter carefully selected the right tools for a job, so the Great Spirit Mata Nui must have had a plan in mind when he chose the six. But what it could be, Onewa had no idea.

Then an awful thought struck him. What if they were not the Matoran meant to become Toa? What if there had been a mistake? An accident? What if one or more of them got Toa stones when they were not meant to do so? What would that mean for Metru Nui?

The idea disturbed him so much that his hand slipped off his proto piton. He caught it, just barely, and decided to stop worrying about what might have been. Things were the way they were. If a crafter got handed a badly made tool to carve, well, he worked with what he was given. Onewa would have to do the same thing.

He was nearing the top now and could see the Great Disk. Getting it out without bringing the slab of protodermis down on top of his head would take skill.

Onewa planted one proto piton, tested to see if it was firm, and then let go of the other. He took hold of the Great Disk and gave a tug, but it wouldn't budge. Another, and another, and still it wasn't going to move.

The Toa of Stone saw only one chance. He was going to have to use both hands. He crawled as far up to the top of the sculpture as he could and let go of the piton. He grabbed the Great Disk with both hands and pulled with all his strength. It gave just a little. Then a little more. One more tug would do it —

It was free!

Onewa felt a split second of triumph. Then he realized the slab was teetering in his direction. That was the good news. He was also falling to the ground, far, far below.

Desperately, he reached out and grabbed one of his pitons. The force of his fall tore it loose from the sculpture, but at least now he had a tool. Now if only he could think of something to do with it.

Down below, Vakama watched Onewa's fall with horror. None of his disks would help in this situation, and melting the slab wouldn't save the Toa of Stone. But there had to be some way his elemental power could help.

Then he remembered something from his lifetime spent around heat and flame. He reached out with his Toa energy and began to heat the air beneath Onewa. Hot air would create an updraft that would slow the Toa's fall, Vakama was almost certain. It wouldn't save him, but it might buy him time to save himself.

Onewa felt his fall slowing slightly as a blanket of warm air surrounded him. He didn't know if it was Vakama giving him this chance or something else, but he was determined not to waste it. He slung his proto piton and caught it on part of the sculpture, twisting his body so he would swing rather than just stop abruptly. The sudden deceleration still felt like it would tear his arm off, but his new Toa strength won out.

He paused to catch his breath and make sure the Great Disk was safe. That's when the shadow fell on him. Onewa looked up to see the massive slab falling right toward him.

He dove headfirst off the sculpture. He tossed his piton ahead of him, felt it catch on the sculpture, and swung around and down. It was now only a short drop to the ground. Onewa hit the sand and rolled, grateful to be back on solid ground.

Then the shadow came again, and he heard Vakama shouting, "Watch out!"

The huge slab of protodermis crashed to the round with a force that sent tremors throughout Po-Metru. When the cloud of sand finally cleared, there stood Onewa, unharmed. Miraculously, the portion of the "mountain" that had come down on him contained the hole that had housed the Great Disk.

From his vantage point, Vakama smiled. Someday, if Onewa allowed it, this would be a wonderful tale to tell.

Vakama, Onewa, Nuhrii and Ahkmou were the first to make it back to the Great Temple. It was Onewa who spotted the squad of Ga-Metru Vahki circling the place.

"What do you think? Could Nokama and Matau be in trouble?" asked Vakama.

Onewa shook his head. "If they had taken two Toa Metru in, the Vahki wouldn't still be here. I'm guessing our friends slipped away and the Vahki are searching the area for them."

"And the other Toa Metru could walk right into their claws. We have to lure them away from here. But what would make Vahki pass up the chance to capture two powerful strangers who appeared in their metru?"

"How about six?" said Onewa, smiling.

"Did I mention this was a bad idea?" asked Nuhrii, trying not to tremble.

"At least eight times," answered Onewa. "It's simple. Just run up to the Vahki and say what we told you."

"Why would they listen to a Ta-Matoran? This is Ga-Metru!"

"Nuhrii, if a Rahi with a slime trail came up to them and told them where to find us, they would listen," said Onewa. "Don't worry. We'd send Ahkmou, but bad things tend to happen whenever he's out my sight."

"Remember, this isn't just about us," said Vakama. "It's for the sake of the whole city."

The Ta-Matoran shrugged. "Yeah. So you keep saying."

Nuhrii dashed out into the avenue and ran straight for the Great Temple. The Vahki immediately flew down and surrounded him. The Toa could not hear what the Matoran was saying, but if he stuck to the script, he was claiming to have seen six strangers on the other end of the metru. They were keeping Matoran from doing their work and generally causing trouble.

As Onewa had expected, that was all the Vahki needed to hear. The Bordakh transformed from bipeds to four-legged creatures, their tools now serving as their front legs. Then they flew off in the direction Nuhrii had pointed. As soon as they were gone, the Ta-Matoran sank to his knees.

Vakama ran over to him. "Good job, Nuhrii."

"You owe me one," said Nuhrii. "You all owe me one."

"Let's hope the city survives long enough for you to collect." Vakama turned at the familiar voice. Nokama was standing behind him with Whenua, Matau, and Nuju, and all were carrying Great Disks. A feeling of relief washed over him — in their first great test, the Toa Metru had succeeded.

"We did as you asked," said Nuju.

"We sought-found the Great Disks," added Matau. "Now what?"

"Tell us how to save the city," said Whenua.

"Ummmm . . . well . . ." Vakama began. His

visions had only shown that the Great Disks were needed to stop the destruction of Metru Nui. The "how" of it had never been revealed.

"Come on, fire-spitter, this was all your idea," snapped Onewa. "We chased all over the city for these things. What are we supposed to do with them?"

"We are supposed to act like Toa," said Nokama. "Vakama put us on the right path. Now we must all decide on the next step. Let us share what we know. Vhisola's researches confirmed what Vakama said — the six Great Disks, used together, can defeat the Morbuzakh. More, it seems there is a single root that is the center of this menace."

"Ehrye showed me records in the Knowledge Tower that refer to a 'king root,'" said Nuju. "It can be recognized by the brown stripe that runs up and down its length."

"But where can it be?" asked Whenua. "It must be huge, to support so many vines over so much distance. Where could such a thing conceal itself?"

"The Archives?" suggested Onewa. "You could hide a Bohrok swarm or three in that place, and still have room for a kolhii disk tournament."

Whenua shook his head. "I'll admit there are a lot of unexplored places down there, but I think we would have noticed evil greenery. What do we know about this thing that might suggest a hiding place?"

"It's strong. It's persistent," Vakama began. "It doesn't seem to like the cold, but thrives in heat. I've never seen anything else survive in a fire pit."

"The Great Furnace," muttered Nuhrii. When the Toa all turned to look at him, he said, "Don't you see? If it loves the heat, what better place to hide?"

"He's right," said the Toa of Fire. "Outside of the fire pits, which are too heavily guarded to provide sanctuary, the Great Furnace is the most significant source of heat in Ta-Metru. If it's driven Matoran away from the area, the Morbuzakh king root could easily conceal itself there."

"Then our course of action is clear," said Nokama. "If there's a chance the root of this menace is in the Great Furnace, then it is to the Great Furnace we shall go. And Vakama will lead us."

"Is that so knowing-wise?" asked Matau. "What makes him any better than the rest?"

Nokama started to answer, but Vakama cut her off. "I'm not interested in being a leader. All I care about is saving the city. Ta-Metru is my home, and I know it better than any of you, so maybe Nokama's right in saying I should be in charge. After we defeat the Morbuzakh, you can all do as you like."

"Too much talking," said Nuju. "Not enough doing. Let's get this over with."

"Any special reason for your hurry?" asked Onewa.

"I hate plants," answered Nuju, as he walked away.

Over their strong objections, the Matoran were going along on the journey to Ta-Metru. Matau had joked that their job would be to keep the king root busy while the Toa waited for the right moment. He assured them that the moment would surely come while at least a few of them were still on their feet. It took Nokama some time to calm them down after that, and she firmly asked Matau to please keep his jokes to himself.

They were traveling along back paths through the city. By now, the Vahki in all six metru had been stirred up and would be watching the chutes. Whenua commented that it was too bad they couldn't change back to Matoran at will, if only to be able to sneak around more effectively.

"You can go back to being a Matoran if you want," Matau had replied. "I like being a Toa-hero!"

By the time they reached the borders of Ga-Metru, Vhisola was looking over her shoulder every few seconds. While the Toa were scanning the air for signs of Vahki, her eyes were fixed on the ground, the shadowy alleys, and anywhere else from which danger might spring.

"What's the matter, Vhisola?" asked No-kama. "You are with six Toa. You will be safe."

"No, I won't," she whispered. "Neither will you, any of you. Don't you know what they say about Morbuzakh vines?"

"Tell me."

"When the Morbuzakh knows you are looking for it —" Vhisola paused and looked around again. Then, in a whisper so soft Nokama could barely hear, she said:

"It comes looking for you."

Just across the northern border of Ta-Metru lay a nearly deserted neighborhood. It had been the site of the first appearances by the Morbuzakh vines. Countless Matoran had disappeared from there, many more had fled for their lives deeper into the metru. Since they entered the area, Vakama had not spoken a word.

"I do not like this place," said Matau, looking around. "It feels cold-dead."

"Where are all the Matoran?" asked Nokama.

"If Ta-Metru is anything like Po-Metru, they are living now with friends or co-workers," answered Onewa. "Some insist on staying near the Vahki hives, believing it to be safer there. If they work near the outskirts, they're careful not to travel alone. Every few moments, they stop working to listen for the approach of a vine."

Whenua frowned. "There was nothing in the past history of Metru Nui to hint such a crisis might occur."

"But something like it was bound to happen," said Nuju. "We relied too much on others to protect us — Toa, Vahki, even Turaga Dume. When something happened they could not handle, all the Matoran could do was run. I could have predicted this."

"Then why didn't you?" asked Vakama, gesturing at the abandoned buildings all around. "Why didn't anyone?"

"I predict we better find a place to hide," broke in Onewa. "There's a Vahki squad up ahead."

"This way." Vakama led his fellow Toa Metru and the six Matoran into a narrow alleyway. Using his flame power, he melted the lock on an old door and shepherded them inside the building.

The heat struck the Toa like a fist. Although no Matoran seemed to be present in the forge, fires still leaped high and smoke made it hard to breathe. Tools were scattered about at the work stations and some items had even been left to melt in the flames.

"They left in a hurry," said Whenua. "Maybe we should do the same."

The Toa of Ice felt something strike his armor and bounce off. It made a sharp sound when it hit, as if it were a pebble. When it happened a second time, Nuju said, "What is that?"

Nokama's keen eyes had spotted where the second object landed. She bent down and scooped it up. It was a round object, roughly a quarter of the diameter of a Kanoka disk. Its outer shell was pitted, extremely hard, and the colors of fire. "It looks like some kind of . . . seed."

Another fell, and then another. That's when the full impact of what she had just said became clear to her. She looked up at the ceiling. It was covered in seeds, which were beginning to fall at a rapid pace. "Oh, Mata Nui protect us," she whispered. "Morbuzakh seeds! It must be!"

Now the Toa Metru were caught in a

downpour. When the seeds struck, tiny vines sprang forth from the shell and wrapped around whatever was closest, hanging on with an unnatural strength.

"We have to get out of here!" Vakama shouted. He took two steps before black-brown tendrils wrapped around his legs, bringing him down hard. More seeds struck him, their vines binding him as effectively as chains. He could see the other Toa struggling, their arms pinned to their sides, their tools out of reach, as more seeds rained down.

The clatter of the shells striking the ground was deafening. Already, the stone floor was covered with a layer of rapidly germinating seeds. The little vines writhed like a nest of baby serpents, striking out to entangle the Toa. Nokama was in the worst shape, with vines covering her from neck to toe and reaching for her Mask of Power.

None of the six Matoran had made it back out the door. They were pinned to the walls by tendrils, like insects caught in a blackened web.

Vakama rolled across the floor, trying to find a sharp-edged fragment of protodermis he could use to saw through the vines. Whenua was on his feet, slamming his body against the wall, evidently trying to stun the plants into letting go.

But it was Nuju who first managed to escape. Nokama's eyes widened as she saw him slice through the vines binding him with an icicle. In mere moments he was free and rushing over to help her. "We have to get the others out of here. Help me!"

While Nuju hurried to untie the other Toa, Nokama used her hydro blades to free the Matoran. Then they all rushed out the door before the vines could grab hold again. Vakama slammed the door shut behind them, stamping on the vines as they tried to slip underneath. "Nuju! Onewa! Bring the building down!"

Onewa called on his elemental energies as Nuju did the same. From one side of the building, a pillar of stone rose into the air. From the other, a pillar of ice took shape. Nodding to each other, both Toa released their control and sent the twin pillars crashing into the roof. Under the weight of rock and ice, the forge collapsed in on itself, burying the plants.

Nokama felt a shudder run through her form. "Do you think that will stop them?"

Vakama shook his head. "Maybe for a little while. You know what this means, don't you?"

"It's reproducing," said Whenua, "and we have no idea how many other seeds might be waiting to sprout. Their roots will link up with the king root and the Morbuzakh will be every-where."

"It could overrun our city-home," Matau said quietly. "Too many vines to stop, too little time."

Vakama checked to make sure his disk launcher was loaded. Then he turned to the group and said, "Let's go. We have a weed to pull."

As they walked, Nokama turned to Nuju. "I appreciate your rescue. But how did you get free?"

"I saw what the seeds were doing to the

others," he said, his eyes looking straight ahead. "So when they began to strike me, I took a deep breath and expanded my chest. Then when I let the breath out, I had just enough slack to move a little. I didn't need my spikes to make something as simple as an icicle."

"That's amazing!"

Nuju shrugged. "I'm from Ko-Metru. We think ahead."

The Great Furnace was not as big or imposing as the Coliseum in the center of Metru Nui. It did not have the feeling of power and mystery that Ga-Metru's Great Temple possessed. But every Ta-Matoran looked at it with awe and wonder. It was a symbol of what made the metru great — the power that turned solid protodermis to molten liquid, and the skill to shape that raw material into the tools Matoran used every day.

Now Vakama stood outside the entrance, staring up at the reddish-black exterior, wondering just what was lurking in the heart of the flame.

"So this is the plan?" asked Onewa in disbelief. "We knock on the front door and ask if the Morbuzakh can come out to play?"

"I am not saying we should listen to all of Vhisola's fears," replied Nokama, making an effort to remain calm. "But if she is right —"

"If she is right, then we are facing more than just a plant," said Matau. "It can think-plan. And it probably already knows we're here."

"Then we won't keep it waiting," said Vakama. "Nuhrii, you and the other Matoran will accompany us inside, but stay back. There is no telling what we will encounter in there."

"One of us should stay out here to run for help, if need be," offered Ahkmou. "I volunteer."

"If we fail," said Onewa, "Metru Nui will be beyond help. Besides, you were so anxious to get the six Great Disks, Ahkmou, I think you should see them in action."

The six Toa Metru looked at each other. The time for talking had passed. Each knew that the challenges they had faced so far could not compare with what they were about to attempt.

No one needed to say that this might be the last adventure for one or more of them. Their good-byes to each other were exchanged in silence.

Vakama melted the lock on the massive door. With a final look at his friends, he opened the gateway to the Great Furnace.

11

Toa and Matoran entered the structure. Just inside the door was a small, bare chamber. Its purpose was to give Matoran a chance to prepare before they proceeded to the inferno inside, or give them a chance to rest after they had spent some time laboring in the furnace. Beyond this chamber was the outer ring, a buffer to keep the intense heat from reaching the outer walls of the building.

Surprisingly, there was no sign of the Morbuzakh here. A moment of panic swept through Vakama. What if they had been wrong? What if the king root was not here?

Then we find it, wherever it hides, he said to himself. *There's no other choice.*

He grasped the handle of the door to the outer ring. Vakama could feel the heat through it. In his mind, he was prepared for almost anything on the other side of that door. But in his heart, he wondered if six new, still untried Toa Metru would have the power to prevail.

Disk launcher ready, Vakama threw open the door and rushed inside. Dim lightstones cast an unsettling glow on the long, narrow chamber. The air was filled with a strange, soft sound that seemed to come from everywhere at once.

"What is that?" asked Vakama. "It sounds like hissing."

"No, not hissing," replied Nokama. "It's . . . whispering."

The Toa Metru stopped dead and looked around. The stone floor of the chamber was broken in numerous places. Growing from the cracks were small, twisted plants, with buds that stank of rot. Close inspection showed the buds were pulsating.

"It's them. The sounds are coming from them," Whenua said. "Are they —"

Onewa stepped carefully, trying to avoid touching any of the plants. "Yes. They're young

Morbuzakh. New vines growing to strangle the city."

The whispering grew louder. The children of the Morbuzakh sensed that they were not alone. A few of the plants began to stir, as if in a breeze. Then more started moving as agitation spread throughout the outer ring.

"We cannot allow these things to grow-thrive," said Matau.

"Let's see how they like a touch of frost." Nuju lowered his crystal spikes and sprayed a fine mist of ice over the plants. As the Toa watched, the ice spread across the entire crop. The plants began to sag beneath the weight, their whispering growing louder, then fainter. Finally, all was silent.

Nokama took a step forward and water splashed around her feet. "Nuju! The heat in here is melting your ice."

"Then I'll make more," said the Toa of Ice. He poured more and more of his energy through his tools, creating layer after layer of frost on top of the plants. Each time the heat of the Great Furnace would melt the ice and the plants would begin to struggle again. Then Nuju would call on more of his power.

The seesaw battle between Toa Metru and the flames of Ta-Metru went on for several long minutes. The other Toa could see that Nuju was weakening. He staggered and would have fallen if Matau had not caught him.

"My power . . . almost gone . . ." gasped Nuju.

This was a mistake, thought Vakama. *Our true struggle is waiting beyond this chamber. We should have saved our power for that. But why would the Morbuzakh leave these young vines undefended?*

The Toa of Fire got his answer in the next moment. Wave after wave of thorns flew from the walls, knifing through the air at the Toa Metru. "Toa! Defend yourselves!" Vakama shouted, hurling firebursts to incinerate the projectiles.

Whenua yelled as one of the thorns grazed his armor. He activated his earthshock drills and began shredding the thorns as they came close.

Across the chamber, Matau was conjuring a wind funnel to blow the thorns away, while Nokama used her hydro blades to parry them. Onewa was having the most trouble, but he stood and let the thorns strike him to buy the Matoran time to seek shelter.

The six Matoran had hit the ground and were scrambling through the melted ice toward the door. Nuhrii glanced up and saw that the hail of thorns was heaviest near the exit. "We'll never make it!"

"We have to," said Ahkmou. "I'm not staying here!"

"Be quiet, Ahkmou!" snapped Tehutti. "We might not be here if it weren't for you. I saw something in the Archives once that might help us. Everyone join hands!"

The other five Matoran did as Tehutti asked. "Now concentrate," the Onu-Matoran said. "We have to focus on our unity. That means you too, Ahkmou!"

At first, their efforts seemed to be have no effect. Then a glow surrounded the six Matoran and their bodies grew hazy and indistinct. There was a sudden, bright burst of light, and when it faded, one Matoran stood where six had been before.

"We are one," the being said in a voice that sounded like a combination of the six Matoran. "We are the Matoran Nui."

The eyes of the merged being scanned the chamber. The Toa Metru were fighting for their lives against the thorn barrage, but making no progress. "We understand now," said the Matoran Nui. "No one Matoran's ambitions are more important than Metru Nui as a whole. We must aid the Toa."

The Matoran Nui darted forward, moving so quickly it dodged the thorns. Then with one blow it demolished the door to the inner chamber. The Toa Metru turned at the noise to stare in amazement at the new being in their midst.

"Go!" said the Matoran Nui. "Defeat the Morbuzakh and save the city! It is what you were meant to do!"

Vakama had a million questions, but no

time to ask any of them. He turned to the other Toa and shouted, "Follow me!"

The six heroes of Metru Nui charged into the heart of the Great Furnace toward what might be their final conflict. The Matoran Nui watched them go, whispering, "Mata Nui protect you all."

Outside of the Great Furnace, the Matoran Nui split apart to become six Matoran again. They blinked and stumbled, drained from their experience. "That was incredible. The power!" said Ehrye.

"Let's do it again," said Vhisola. "Think of all we could do for our city."

Ahkmou shook his head and backed away. "No. No. No way. If you five want to risk your lives, go ahead, but count me out. I'm looking out for what's most important: me."

"Then go," said Tehutti. "If unity, duty, and destiny mean nothing to you, run back to Po-Metru, Ahkmou."

The Po-Matoran laughed. "We'll see each other again. Don't worry. And then we will see just whose destiny will win out."

With that, Ahkmou turned and fled into the shadows.

The Toa Metru stood in the midst of a nightmare.

The massive inner chamber of the Great Furnace had been transformed into a sanctuary for the king root of the Morbuzakh. Dominating the room was a huge, thick, winding stalk that extended from the ground all the way to the rooftop. The winding stripe that ran down its length marked it as the source of the Morbuzakh plague.

Branches extended all along the root, entwining themselves with the masonry of the walls and floors. The king root had truly become a part of the Great Furnace. The Toa Metru could imagine each of those branches extending beyond the furnace, with multiple vines sprouting from them to threaten Metru Nui.

Waves and waves of intense heat washed over the Toa. Already Nuju and Whenua were beginning to weaken. Vakama turned to the Toa of Water, saying, "Nokama, you must use your power to try to keep us cool. Can you do it?"

"I don't know," replied Nokama. "I will do my best."

The Toa of Water concentrated, calling on her energies to condense the moisture in the air into a cooling mist. It was an enormous drain, with the heat taking its toll on her as well. She could not help but wonder how long her strength would hold out, and what would happen if she fell.

Vakama felt overwhelmed. The king root was far bigger and more frightening than he had ever dreamed. How could six disks, even Great Disks, bring such a monstrosity down? But what choice did they have?

"Ready the disks," he said. "We will strike together and —"

"Noooo!" The voice cracked like lightning in the minds of the Toa. "You will not dessssstroy the Morbuzakh!"

"What? Who was that?" said Onewa, looking around.

"It wasssss I!" the voice boomed again.

"Mata Nui," whispered Nokama. "It's the Morbuzakh — it speaks!"

"Yessss, I ssspeak. I sssspeak. I think. I feel. And Metru Nui sssshall be mine!"

Vakama could see no eyes or mouth anywhere on the root. It was not truly speaking, the Toa were simply hearing its thoughts. Worse, they could sense its feelings — an overwhelming hunger to possess the city and drive away anything that was not Morbuzakh. There was more there as well, traces of another intelligence, but they were too vague for the Toa to comprehend.

"My armssss extend to every part of thissss city," the Morbuzakh continued. "I am in the furnacesss, the canalsss, the chutesss. The Matoran live and work only because I choossse to let them. But if they anger me —"

A vine suddenly shot out of the wall, wrapped around a pipe, and crushed it to dust. "Firsst, I will drive the Matoran away from the outskirtsss of the city, so they cannot essscape. Then I will claim this place as my own. Those who ssssurvive can ssserve the Morbuzakh, or perisssh."

The full horror of what they were hearing struck the Toa then. This was no mere over-grown menace, like the wild Rahi beasts that sometimes appeared in the city. The Morbuzakh was intelligent, cunning, and evil beyond anything they had ever imagined. None of them doubted that, if allowed to spread unchecked, this thing would do what it promised. Metru Nui would fall and the Matoran would become slaves of the Morbuzakh, or worse.

So shocked were the Toa Metru that none of them noticed a vine creeping up behind Whenua. It struck amazingly fast, ripping the Great Disk from the Toa's grasp and snaking up toward the ceiling. Whenua shouted and grabbed the vine, which lifted him high into the air.

Nuju ran, leaped, and caught Whenua's legs. He, too, was yanked off his feet and up toward the ceiling. The Morbuzakh vine whipped around violently in an effort to shake the Toa off. "Hang on!" shouted Nuju.

"Thanks! That was my plan!" said Whenua. "Did you come up here just to tell me that?"

Down below, vines had wrapped themselves around Vakama and Onewa, but Matau had proven too fast for them. The Toa of Air darted across the floor, heading straight for the king root. "Morbuzakh, meet a Toa-hero!"

Before Matau's startled eyes, a new vine grew out of the root. Before he could change direction, the vine swatted him out of the air and sent him crashing into the wall.

Nokama, still straining to maintain her power, watched as Vakama's fire and Onewa's stone failed to make the vines break their grip. Above, Nuju had called upon his ice power but it was too weak to free him and Whenua.

This is all wrong, she thought. *We are all fighting individual battles, instead of working as a team. There has to be a way to stop this thing!*

Ignoring the possible consequences, Nokama suddenly dropped her efforts to keep the Toa cool amid the awful heat. She fired a stream of water up toward the vine that held Whenua's Great Disk, shouting, "Nuju! Freeze this!"

The Toa of Ice did as she asked, forming the curving stream of water into an ice hook. Reaching out and grabbing it, he used the ice to pull the end of the vine close. "Whenua! Now!"

Whenua thrust his earthshock drill forward and sliced through the vine. The portion holding the Great Disk fell away and plunged toward the ground as the vine writhed.

Nokama glanced at Matau, who had finally regained his feet. Her eyes met his and she knew he was ready. He raised his aero slicers and hurled a blast of air at the falling vine, blowing it toward Nokama. The Toa of Water caught it on the fly, tore the vine loose, and held the Great Disk up proudly.

"Your first defeat, monster!" she shouted at the king root. "But hardly your last!"

"You can delay me, but not defeat me!" The Morbuzakh's voice sounded like a swarm of metallic hornets. "I am a part of Metru Nui now. I am thisss city, and it isss me!"

"Then we will tear you out by the roots, Morbuzakh!" Vakama shouted. "One way or another, your reign ends today!"

The vine holding Vakama swung him close to the body of the king root. Vakama took the opportunity to toss fireballs at the Morbuzakh, but the plant simply absorbed them. "Yesssss," said the Morbuzakh. "More! Fire feedssss me!"

Whenua looked down at Matau, who nodded. Then the Toa of Earth let go of the vine, sending Nuju and himself plummeting toward the ground. When they were midway through their fall, Matau sent two mighty gusts of wind toward them. The wind caught the two Toa and flung them across the chamber right at the vines holding Vakama and Onewa.

Toa of Ice and Toa of Earth slammed into the vines. The impact freed the two trapped Toa, who dropped to the ground. They had no chance to rest, however — Morbuzakh vines were now coming from every side, trying to grab the Toa or their Great Disks.

Now began a desperate struggle, for the Toa Metru were not facing just one powerful, if immobile, enemy. They were fighting the thousand "arms" of the Morbuzakh, each as strong as the last, which struck and then slithered away. Toa tools flashed. Fire, ice, water, stone, earth, and cyclones filled the air. But for every vine the Toa struck down, three more rose to take its place.

Eventually, the Toa began to tire. Without extensive practice in controlling and rationing their elemental energies, their powers began to run low. Little by little, the vines drove them away from the king root, growing bolder as they sensed the Toa slowing down.

"You cannot sssstop me," hissed the Morbuzakh. "You have not the ssstrength. That isss all right. Too weak to be heroesss, perhapsss, but you will ssstill make excellent ssslavesss."

"He's right," said Vakama. "We can't win this way."

Onewa drove off another vine and looked at the Toa of Fire in disbelief. "This was your idea, and now you're quitting? What kind of a Toa are you?"

"Stop fighting," Vakama said flatly. "It's our only chance."

"You have gone around the chute," said Matau. "We stop hard-fighting and the vines will overwhelm us and drag us to the —" The Toa of Air suddenly stopped and a broad smile appeared on his face. "For a fire-spitter, Vakama, sometimes you can be almost as quick-smart as a Le-Matoran."

Vakama checked to make sure that all the Toa had their Great Disks in their hands. Then he shouted, "Now!" As one, they dropped their Toa tools and stopped struggling against the vines.

At first, the Morbuzakh did not seem to know how to react. When the king root spoke in their minds, there was confusion in its tone. "You would not sssurrender. Thisss is sssome trick. My vinesss could crusssh you where you ssstand!"

"Then do it," said Nokama. "Don't just talk about it."

"Maybe when we are done here, we could transplant this thing to Ga-Metru," Whenua suggested. "You know, add it to the garden near the canals. Ga-Matoran could climb it and build root-houses."

"As long as it stops speaking," said Nuju. "There is nothing I dislike more than a talkative shrub."

"Do what you like, Morbuzakh," snapped Onewa. "I would rather be fed to the Great Furnace than live in a city run by an obnoxious, foul-smelling, overgrown pile of vegetable matter good for nothing but clogging canals."

The Morbuzakh's bellow was so loud the Toa thought sure their heads would split open. Six vines shot around and wrapped around the heroes' waists, hauling them through the air toward the king root. The pressure of the vines was tremendous, threatening to squeeze the air out of the Toa's lungs.

"Before you ssserve, you will sssuffer!"

Vakama held up his Great Disk as the other Toa did the same. "No, Morbuzakh. You have had your season. The time for the harvest has come!"

Pure power flashed from the six Great Disks, blindingly bright bands of energy that twisted around each other. Lightning flashed wherever two bands touched, striking at the vines that reached for the Toa. Then the energies blended together, forming a sphere in mid-air that moved slowly and inexorably toward the Morbuzakh.

Desperately, the Morbuzakh tried to escape its own end. It writhed, the sheer power of its vines pulling down the walls of the Great Furnace. Masonry rained down from the ceiling as the plant's upper branches tried to batter their way to freedom. Great blocks of protodermis crumbled and fell into the flames, consumed in an instant, and still the Morbuzakh struggled. It had truly become one with this fortress of fire, and now both were about to fall.

Taking advantage of the distraction, the Toa fought their way free of the vines that imprisoned them. Vakama looked up and saw that power no longer flowed from his Great Disk, nor from any of the others. But the sphere still existed, growing larger and larger every moment.

"Toa, we have to go! Now!" he shouted. "The Morbuzakh will bring the Great Furnace down upon us!"

Then came a sound the Toa Metru would remember for the rest of their lives: the sound of the king root screaming.

That put an end to any arguments there might have been. Instead, the Toa raced for the exit to the outer chamber, pausing only to pick up their tools. They did not stop running until they were far from the Great Furnace and the thing that had dwelled inside.

Only Vakama dared to look back. Through the crumbling walls, he could see that the energy sphere now encompassed the king root. Its walls had sliced through the multitude of vines, the high branches, and the deep roots that anchored the Morbuzakh in the ground. All around, the plant growth that had menaced Metru Nui was writhing and crumbling to dust.

The king root hung suspended in the air now, trapped within the energy sphere. Cut off from the ground below and from its branches and vines, the root could no longer draw energy from the fires of Ta-Metru or feed it to the rest of the plant. It was alive, but isolated, a creature once connected with all of Metru Nui and now utterly alone. Eventually, its howls of rage began to fade away in the minds of the Toa, replaced by the sound of their own thoughts.

The Great Furnace was now nothing but rubble and flames. The sphere glowed amid the wreckage as the struggles of the king root ceased. Then, as suddenly as it had appeared, the energy was gone. The king root struck the ground with a resounding crash and then crumbled to nothing before the Toa of Fire's astounded eyes.

* * *

All around the city, Matoran looked on in wonder as the Morbuzakh vines turned to dust. Soon, there would be no sign of the plant left, except for the damage it had done. But the defeat of the Morbuzakh would not bring back all the Matoran who had vanished since the vines had first appeared in Metru Nui.

Back at the ruins of the Great Furnace, Nokama looked at Vakama. "Is it really over?"

"Yes," said the Toa of Fire. "With the king root gone, the rest of the Morbuzakh should soon follow. We have passed our first test as Toa Metru."

"Then why are we standing here?" asked Matau. "Let's bring these ever-powerful disks to the Coliseum and tell the world we are Toa-heroes!"

The six Toa Metru looked at each other and smiled. Matau's idea sounded like a good one. After all, despite their differences, they had found the Great Disks, defeated the Morbuzakh, and saved their city. As they walked away from the site of their first great victory, they knew they were no longer the Matoran they had been . . . or even the new Toa they had become . . .

They were heroes of Metru Nui.

EPILOGUE

Turaga Vakama rose, signaling that his tale had come to an end. Takanuva, the Toa of Light, stood as well, smiling. "What a wonderful story!" he said. "The six of you started out as Matoran, just like I did, and became heroes. I bet the whole city turned out to cheer for you!"

Vakama chuckled. "You are attaching a happy ending to my tale, Takanuva, because you wish there to be one. But there is much more to tell."

"You had a vision when you first became a Toa," said Tahu, Toa of Fire. "A vision of disaster. Did defeating the Morbuzakh spare the city from that terrible event?"

"It spared the city from the Morbuzakh," said Turaga Vakama. "We believed that was enough. Our world was very simple, Tahu, with good on one side and evil on the other."

"What's wrong with that?" asked Onua, Toa of Earth. "I mean, we Toa challenged the Rahi and many other threats to this island. We fought for justice and to defend the Matoran and their villages. We stood up for the light and defeated the darkness that rose against us."

"You are very wise, Onua," said Vakama. "But you have only the wisdom of your experience. That is why you are here now — to gain the wisdom of mine."

There was an uncomfortable silence, broken finally by Takanuva. "It's late. I suppose we should leave Turaga Vakama to his rest. There will be time tomorrow for another tale. There is another tale to tell, isn't there, Turaga?"

"Oh, yes, Takanuva," said Vakama. *A dark one indeed,* he added to himself.

The Toa departed, all but Gali, Toa of Water. She had always been sensitive to others' moods, and she could tell that Vakama was troubled. It was more than just confronting the memories of his past. It seemed as if there were some terrible secret he knew he must share, but dreaded doing so.

"Why do you tell these tales, Turaga?" she asked softly. "Is it only to prepare us for the journey to Metru Nui, and what we may encounter there?"

"You already know the answer," he said, "or you would not ask the question. No, there is a great difference between the Toa Nuva that you are, and the Toa Metru that we Turaga were long ago. Your enemies hide in the shadows, but you know they are there. They make no effort to hide the darkness in their hearts. For us, it was . . . different."

"But you were strong," she said. "You triumphed. You had the three virtues to guide you — Unity, Duty, Destiny."

"Yes, we six had done our duty, we believed," Vakama said, with a trace of sadness in his voice. "And we felt certain we had achieved our destiny. But our unity? That still remained to be forged in the fires of danger, far greater danger than we had known before."

Vakama leaned on his firestaff. Not for the first time, Gali found it hard to believe that the Turaga had once been a mighty Toa Metru. "You see, Toa of Water, we believed that we knew all we needed to know to be heroes. We could challenge an enemy, outwit it, defeat it, save Matoran, even save a city. Oh, we still needed training in our powers and we still had to master our masks. But being a hero? There was nothing left for us to learn there, we felt sure."

Vakama looked at Gali. She understood now that his eyes had seen a greater darkness than any Toa Nuva could comprehend. *What happened on Metru Nui?* she wondered.

"We thought we knew it all. But we were wrong, Gali, so very wrong. Our true lessons were about to begin."